W9-CTD-768

Larry Harmon's T.V.

BOZO

and the
Hide 'n' Seek Elephant

by William Johnston

BOZO THE CLOWN

™ LARRY HARMON PICTURES CORPORATION

illustrated by
Allan Hubbard
and
Milli Jancar

glb
GOLDEN PRESS
Western Publishing Company, Inc.
Racine, Wisconsin

© 1968 Larry Harmon Pictures Corporation
All rights reserved. Produced in U.S.A.
by Western Publishing Company, Inc.

Fifth Printing, 1975

GOLDEN, A LITTLE GOLDEN BOOK®, and GOLDEN PRESS®
are trademarks of Western Publishing Company, Inc.

"Bozo! Bozo!" Butch called. "Queenie the Elephant is missing — and she's due in the center ring in half an hour."

"Golly tamale! That's bad!" said Bozo. "Is she hiding again?"

Butch nodded. "Queenie and Big Freda had words. Queenie's feelings got hurt. Just like always, she went off and hid."

"And just like always, I'll bet she's pretending to be a 'something' she really isn't," said
Bozo. "Well, don't get all discombooberated,
Butchy-boy. We'll take a little hippety-hop hop
and find that little elephant."

Faster than a firefly can flit, Bozo and Butch popped into the Bozomobile. As they took off, Butch pointed to a big poster. "Look, Bozo. There's her picture — life-size, star of the circus. People will be mighty disappointed when she isn't there."

Bozo just glanced at the poster. He was thinking aloud. "Now let me see . . . once she hid out in a pasture, looking like a big rock, and once she pretended to be a school bus —"

Suddenly Bozo broke off. A treetop below them was twitching strangely.

"Look there, Butchy-boy," he said. "It's worth a try. I'm going to land."

"Yeah, Bozo," said Butch as they settled to the ground. "But what would Queenie pretend to be in a forest?"

"Think!" said Bozo. "That little elephant's legs are like tree trunks. Why, she could've covered herself with branches and be hiding out as a whole clumpety clump of trees."

Bozo and Butch hopped out of the Bozomobile and trotted into the forest.

They walked among the trees, calling, "Where are you, Queenie?"

But not one of those trees had an elephant trunk, or elephant ears, or elephant eyes. "Queenie may be pretending to be a 'something else,'" Bozo said, "but I don't think it's a forest."

"Fifteen minutes to go, Bozo," said Butch as
they took off. "What now?"

Bozo thought hard. "Let's hippety hop past
that poster again," he said. "Maybe it'll give
us an idea."

And so they flew back to the circus and dipped
low for another look.

Suddenly Bozo snapped his fingers. He pointed at Queenie's trunk. "The spittin' image of a fire hose," he said. "Could be our Queenie is hiding out as —"

"A fire engine!" shouted Butch. "Like the time she painted herself orange and hid among the school buses."

Faster than a fish with greased fins, they flew to the nearest firehouse. There they nosed in and out among the fire engines, calling, "Queenie! Oh, Queenie! Where are you hiding? Come out, wherever you are!"

The fire engines did have big fire hoses, but they were all for real fires. Not one of them had an elephant trunk or answered to the name of Queenie.

Suddenly the Fire Chief appeared. "What's going on here?" he asked, suspiciously.

"Nothing, Chief," Bozo answered, "but a little old elephant hunt."

"She's painted red," added Butch, "and goes *ding* when the alarm sounds."

The Chief thought they were poking fun at him. His face turned a fiery red.

"Hokey-smokey!" Bozo exclaimed. "Let's go, Butchy-boy, before the Chief goes up in smoke."

"Five more minutes," Butch moaned as they climbed back into the Bozomobile, "and there'll be a tentful of sad people at the circus."

Bozo's forehead was crinkled up in a thoughtful frown as he headed the Bozomobile back to the circus. But then, as they came in sight of the poster once more, his face lit up.

"Butchy-boy!" he shouted. "I've got me a brainy brainstorm! Yes, sir-ee-dy, that little elephant cooked up a tricky trick this time. Come on!"

He landed the Bozomobile near the poster and hopped out.

"Bozo! Wait!" called Butch. "What *is* Queenie this time? A giant-sized mouse?"

"No, sir-ee-dy!" Bozo replied as they neared the poster. "That smart little elephant is pretending to be — herself!"

With that Bozo strode to the poster.

He bowed low. "Hey-dee-hoh and hi-dee-hoo
— and a howdy to *you*, Miss Queenie," he said,
and he pulled the trunk on the "picture."
Queenie trumpeted loudly.

"Our missing Queenie," Bozo said proudly, "has been standing in front of this poster all the time, pretending to be her own picture."

Well! Big Freda said she was sorry for having words with Queenie. And Queenie said she was sorry she made everyone worry. And the circus boss was so glad to have Queenie there on time that he ordered an extra bale of hay for dessert.

"Butchy-boy," Bozo said as they watched Queenie enter the ring just in time to do her act, "this has been a real handy-dandy little adventure."

"It has?" asked Butch.

"You bet your boots!" said Bozo.

"Why do you say that?" Butch asked his friend.

"Why," exclaimed Bozo, "if it ever happens now that somebody needs to hide an elephant, we're the only ones in the whole ding-dong world who know HOW . . . dee ho-ho-ho!"

And Bozo sat down to watch the show, chuckling to himself.